SpongeBob JokePants

Stephen Hillenburg

Based on the TV series *SpongeBob SquarePants®*
created by Stephen Hillenburg as seen on Nickelodeon®

SIMON SPOTLIGHT
An imprint of Simon & Schuster Children's Publishing Division
1230 Avenue of the Americas, New York, New York, 10020

Manufactured in the United States of America
First Edition
2 4 6 8 10 9 7 5 3 1

ISBN 0-689-85568-0

SpongeBob JokePants

by David Lewman

Simon Spotlight/Nickelodeon

New York   London   Toronto   Sydney   Singapore

What would you call Gary if he lived on a farm?

"The Farmer in the Shell."

What's SpongeBob's favorite kind of knot?

The square knot.

What kind of shoes does SpongeBob wear?

Penny loofahs.

5

Was Squidward mad when
SpongeBob jumped on his mop?

Yes, he flew off the handle.

Why couldn't Plankton pay
for his Krabby Patty?

He was a little short.

What side order does Sandy always get with her Krabby Patty?

Squirrelly fries.

What does SpongeBob do when Squidward drops food?

He goes on a mopping spree!

What does Mr. Krabs like best about SpongeBob?

His buck teeth.

How does Mr. Krabs start every bedtime story?

"Once upon a dime . . ."

8

What's Mr. Krabs's favorite kind of bread?

Pumper-nickel.

What kind of nuts does Mr. Krabs like the best?

Cash-ews.

What do you see when Mr. Krabs's daughter smiles?

Her Pearly whites.

9

Why did SpongeBob fail his boating test?

He forgot to fasten his sea belt.

Mrs. Puff: Knock-knock.
SpongeBob: Who's there?
Mrs. Puff: Teach.
SpongeBob: Teach who?
Mrs. Puff: Teach yourself
to drive—I give up!

RULES
of the
ROAD

What does every restaurant get when SpongeBob's behind the wheel?

A drive-through.

11

Patrick: What do sponges
play at their
birthday parties?
SpongeBob: Musical squares.

What game does SpongeBob
play with his shoes?

Hide-and-squeak.

Why did SpongeBob tear himself in half at the end of the party?
Because Sandy said it was time to split.

Why did SpongeBob wash the reef?
He was practicing good coral hygiene.

Is Plankton nice to the reefs around Bikini Bottom?

No, he's rotten to the coral.

How do angelfish greet each other?

"Halo!"

Why does Sandy's fur stand up on end whenever Plankton's around?

He rubs her the wrong way.

14

Where do Sandy and SpongeBob practice their karate?

In choppy water.

Sandy: What kind of pizza do they serve at the bottom of the ocean?

SpongeBob: Deep dish.

What kind of earrings does Sandy's mom wear?

Mother-of-squirrel.

15

What do you get when you cross a squid and a dog?

An octo-pooch.

What do you get when
you cross a hunting dog,
a seagull, and a bumblebee?

A bee-gull.

Why can't Sandy play on Patrick's basketball team?

Because he's on an all-star team.

Why did Patrick stare at a mirror with his mouth open?

Squidward told him to watch his tongue.

What's salty and feels good on a sunburn?

The Pacific Lotion.

Is Patrick happy with the way he looks?

Yes, he's tickled pink!

What makes Patrick grouchy?

Waking up on the wrong side of the rock.

Why did SpongeBob chop
the joke book in half?

Squidward told him
to cut the comedy.

What's the most popular
hobby in Bikini Bottom?

Damp collecting!

How did Squidward do in
the hundred-yard dash?

He won by a nose.

What kind of ocean bird can't fly, can't swim, and can't catch fish?

A peli-can't.

What did SpongeBob yell when he dressed up as a bear?

"I'm Teddy!"

Squidward: Why does Gary meow?

SpongeBob: Because he doesn't know how to bark!

Patrick: Can you catch
a jellyfish with
a horn?
SpongeBob: Sure, if it's
a clari-net.

Patrick: Can you catch
a jellyfish with
a puppet?
SpongeBob: Sure, if it's
a mario-net.

Patrick: Can you catch a jellyfish with your hair?
SpongeBob: Sure, if you're a bru-net.

Patrick: Can you catch a jellyfish with your hands?
SpongeBob: Sure, but you'll get stung.

23

Why can't seahorses agree on new rules?

They always vote neigh.

What's the difference between SpongeBob and a gold chain?

One's a yellow necklace, and the other's yellow and neck-less.

If Sandy were a tree, what kind would she be?

A fur tree.

SpongeBob: Why can't an eel ever win an argument?

Sandy: It doesn't have a leg to stand on.

Why did SpongeBob practice his karate at the Krusty Krab?

He thought he was supposed to punch in and punch out.

Where do crabs take classes?

Claw school.

What's Mr. Krabs's favorite chore?

Taking out the cash.

Does SpongeBob have a good
time at work?

Yes, he's the life
of the patty.

**What do Krabby Patties and
long hair have in common?**

They both fit in a bun.

Patrick: What do jellyfish
eat for breakfast?
SpongeBob: Floatmeal!

SpongeBob: What has two big
claws and is very
messy?
Patrick: A slobster!

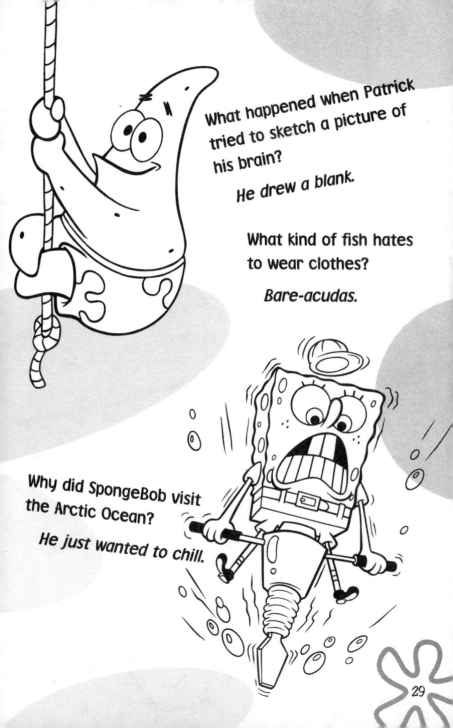

What happened when Patrick tried to sketch a picture of his brain?

He drew a blank.

What kind of fish hates to wear clothes?

Bare-acudas.

Why did SpongeBob visit the Arctic Ocean?

He just wanted to chill.

Mermaid Man: How did the other students do on Mrs. Puff's test?
Barnacle Boy: They sailed through it.

Why didn't the jellyfish do well in Mrs. Puff's class?

He kept drifting off.

Why won't SpongeBob drive to Patrick's house?

He doesn't want to rock the boat.

What happened when SpongeBob ate mashed potatoes in Mrs. Puff's class?

He got a lump in his boat.

Patrick: Do you like barnacles?
SpongeBob: They're growing on me.

What did Mrs. Puff do at the end of SpongeBob's lesson?

She went on a long inflation.

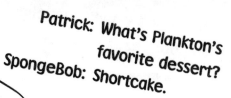

Patrick: What's Plankton's favorite dessert?

SpongeBob: Shortcake.

If Patrick's best friend were a dessert, what kind would he be?

Sponge cake.

Why would Mr. Krabs like to be a bowl of chocolate ice cream?

Because it's very rich.

Patrick: Who haunts the seven seas but never vacuums?

SpongeBob: The Flying Dustman!

Mermaid Man: What does it take to get into a fish choir?

Barnacle Boy: You have to be able to carry a tuna.

Why did Patrick pull the ship with a rope?

He'd heard it was a tugboat.

33

Where would SpongeBob live
after an earthquake?
In a pineapple upside-down
house.

What do you call someone who
just sits around blowing into a
shell?

A conch potato!

Why didn't SpongeBob's pants
fall down during the hurricane?

He was saved by the belt.

Sandy: Why didn't the boy penguin ask the girl penguin out on a date?

SpongeBob: He got cold feet.

How is Sandy able to get around Bikini Bottom without getting wet?

She has her dry-fur's license.

Why did the police arrest Gary?

He was found at the scene of the slime.

Knock-knock.
Who's there?
Hatch.
Hatch who?
Gesundheit!

Squidward: Knock-knock.
SpongeBob: Who's there?
Squidward: Claire.
SpongeBob: Claire who?
Squidward: Clarinets sound
             beautiful,
             don't they?

Why does Mr. Krabs have so many clocks in his house?

Because time is money.

Why does Mr. Krabs like to mop up?

Because inside every bucket, there's a buck.

Why did SpongeBob put his ear to the cash register?

Because Mr. Krabs told him, "Money talks."

Was Mr. Krabs mad when SpongeBob dropped the butter?

No, he let it slide.

What do you call Mr. Krabs when he's holding a coin?

A penny-pincher.

39

How does SpongeBob get exercise?

He does deep-sea bends.

Why did the quilt refuse to go to Bikini Bottom?

She didn't want to be a wet blanket.

What does SpongeBob
sleep in?

His under-square.

Where do sea cows
sleep at night?

In the barn-acle.

Squidward: Why do starfish get up
in the middle of the night?

SpongeBob: They have to twinkle.

How do you save jellyfish from drowning?

Throw them some life preserves.

Why couldn't Patrick understand what the jellyfish was saying?

It was way over his head.

Why did SpongeBob toss the sandwich at Patrick?

He wanted to throw him a surprise patty.

SpongeBob: What has horns, four legs,
and is made out of soap?
Sandy: A bubbalo!

When is SpongeBob like a battery?

When he gets all charged up!

Why doesn't SpongeBob go to the barber?

He doesn't like to cut corners.

Why do SpongeBob and Sandy surf so well together?

They're on the same wavelength.

What did Sandy say when she finished gathering acorns?

"That's all, oaks!"

How does Sandy feel about SpongeBob?

She's nuts about him!

What's SpongeBob's favorite last-minute Halloween costume?

Swiss cheese.

The End.